National Family Partnership is pleased to present *Stinky The Skunk,* the tale of a lonely skunk who uses his own special skill to come to the rescue of the other woodland animals. They, in turn, creatively find a way around the obstacle in their relationship with Stinky. In the tradition of *The Red Ribbon* and *Robbie Rabbit,* storyteller John Lasne has created a warm and inviting fable about friendship and about appreciating diversity.

Stinky the Skunk hid under a bush
watching the animals play.
He knew if he tried to join in their fun
they'd tell him to just go away.

You see, Stinky was stinky 'cause he was a skunk.
(He surely wasn't a rose.)
And when he roamed near other critters
you'd see them grab for their nose.

"We smelled you coming before you arrived!"
they said when he tried to fit in.
"We don't want you playing here,
so don't come 'round again."

Poor ol' Stinky, he'd tuck his thick tail
and waddle off for home.
He figured he'd always be just a skunk
and would always be alone.

But his momma said he was a fine young skunk,
a shiny, handsome lad.
"Be proud of who you are," she said,
"and don't you feel so sad."

But Stinky stayed lonely, watching the others
play their games together.
Until the day the bobcat came,
and changed his world forever.

He was a sneaky bobcat, with sharp, long teeth,
and when he walked there wasn't a sound.
The animals trembled, unable to move,
anchored to the ground.

Too scared to move a single muscle
stood the chipmunk, squirrel and rabbit.
While the bobcat looked them up and down
and snarled–an evil habit.

"Hmmm. Oh, yes. Ah ha," he hissed.
"Have you noticed I've grown much thinner?
I think I'll return tomorrow at six
and eat you all for dinner!

"Don't try to hide, my delicious friends,
you'll still be on my plate.
So tomorrow at six, dinner for one.
Let's consider it a date."

He slipped into the dark, deep woods
and the animals made such cries
they didn't notice Stinky walk up
'til he said, "Wait a minute, you guys.

"I've got a plan to save your skins,
but you gotta do what I say.
Now line up there and close your eyes,
and I'll give you a little spray!"

They shook their heads and said, "No chance!
We don't want to be all smelly!"
"Well maybe," said Stinky, "you'd rather wind up
inside that bobcat's belly."

They saw Stinky's point and all decided
that what he said was true.
So they each got sprayed with smelly stuff
to stay off the bobcat's menu.

The next day at six the bobcat returned,
a hungry look in his eyes.
There stood all the animal friends
with their awfully smelly surprise.

"I'll eat you first," he sneered at the squirrel
until he got downwind.
"Awww! The smell! Who could eat that?
No problem . . . I'll eat your friend!"

So he walked toward the rabbit and said out loud
"You'll do just fine, I think."
Then he took another step and howled,
"Good grief! What is that stink?

"Forget rabbit! Forget squirrel! I'll just
nibble tasty chipmunk."
But when he got too close to his meal
it smelled too much like skunk.

"I'd rather go hungry!" the bobcat cried.
"You've ruined my appetite!"
He crept away into the woods
and disappeared from sight.

"Hooray! We're saved! And thanks to Stinky
we'll live another day!
Let's run right over to his house
and ask him out to play."

But then they stopped dead in their tracks,
the rabbit, squirrel and chipmunk.
They remembered what they'd just forgot:
how badly Stinky stunk!

But it shouldn't matter one single bit
if they truly wanted a friend.
That's when chipmunk had a great idea,
which required a tight clothespin.

After their baths, they found three pins
and pinched their noses tight.
They couldn't smell a single thing!
(But that was the point, right?)

"Stinky, Stinky, come out to play!
Come out and be our friend!"
And Stinky scampered through his door.
He'd never be lonely again!

The animals learned a lesson that day,
a lesson they love to tell.
About the time they became best friends
with a skunk they couldn't smell.

So if you truly want a friend
to put inside your heart,
you'll overcome the differences
keeping you apart.

Ol' Stinky couldn't change his smell
(he'd never lose his scent).
But the animals discovered *they* could change,
and gain a brand new friend.

So now the animals jump and play
and fill the woods with laughter.
Three wear clothespins, one still smells,
but they all live happily ever after.

Stinky The Skunk is a fitting addition to the line of drug prevention materials produced by National Family Partnership (NFP). When children learn to celebrate the differences in others and in themselves—and when they find acceptance— prevention has begun.

For information about NFP's books or drug prevention materials, call National Family Partnership at 314-845-1933 or write: 11159-B South Towne Square, St. Louis, MO 63123-7824. For information about John Lasne or to schedule a storytelling event, call 864-322-5594.

National Family Partnership is a non-profit organization whose mission is to promote healthy, drug-free youth through prevention and education. NFP is the official sponsor of National Red Ribbon Celebration (October 23 – 31).

Our special thanks to the *Elks* , whose contribution through their Drug Awareness Program, a project of the Elks National Foundation, helped make *Stinky The Skunk* possible.

Creative concept, design and text are by Greg & Greg Advertising, Inc., of Greenville, South Carolina. Illustrations are by Joel Wilkinson.